A GOLDEN BOOK • NEW YORK

randomhousekids.com
ISBN 978-1-5247-1720-9
T#: 506523
MANUFACTURED IN CHINA
10 9 8 7 6 5 4 3 2 1

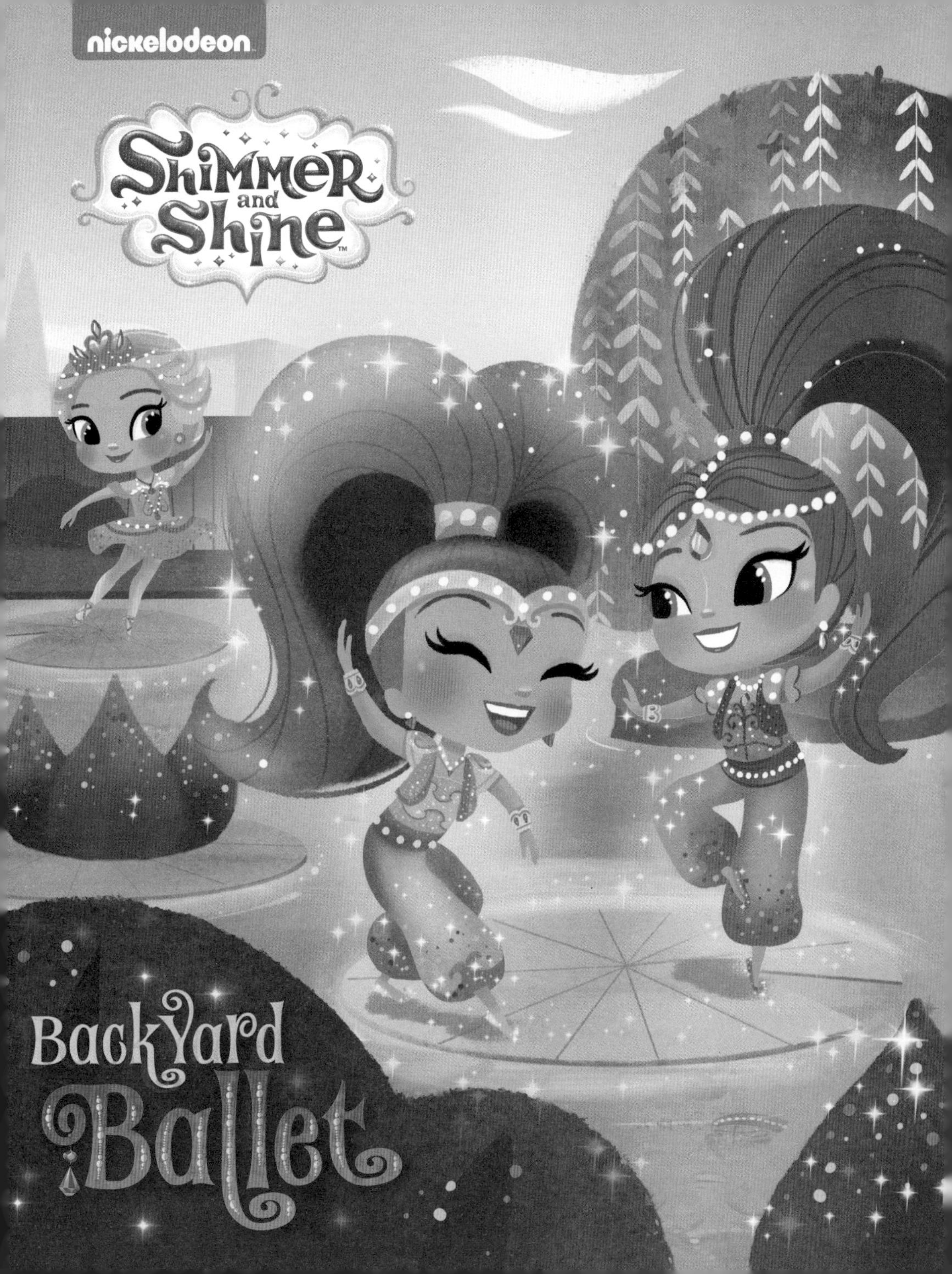
nickelodeon
Shimmer and Shine™
Backyard Ballet

eah and Zac were twirling and leaping around Leah's living room. They had just seen *Swan Lake,* and they were practicing to put on their own ballet!

Leah spun and lost her balance. Zac crashed into the couch!

"I guess we need more practice," Leah giggled.

Zac grinned. "How about you practice spinning and I practice leaping? Later we can dance *Swan Lake* together!"

After Zac left to practice on his own, Leah sighed.
"If only I could dance like the real Swan Queen."
Suddenly, she had an idea!

Leah summoned Shimmer and Shine, twin genies-in-training who could grant her three wishes a day.

"I wish I was the Swan Queen!" Leah declared.

"*Boom, Zahramay! First wish of the day!*" chanted Shine.

Leah found herself dressed as the Swan Queen from the ballet—but with six loud swans as royal subjects!

"I was hoping to spin like the *ballerina* Swan Queen, not be the actual queen of six swans!" she said.

Shine frowned. "Oh, sounds like I made a mistake."

Leah smiled. "It's okay, Shine. Sometimes mistakes happen. Maybe these swans won't get in the way of spinning practice!"

But having six swans in Leah's living room
turned into a giant honking disaster!

Leah had to get the swans outside before they destroyed the whole house.

"I wish the swans would follow me!" she cried. Shimmer jangled her magic bracelets. *"Boom, Zahramay! Second wish of the day!"*

Now the swans followed Leah's every move,
whether she turned her head or hopped on one foot.
Though it wasn't what she had wished for, she loved it!
The swans lined up and followed her to the backyard.

Leah had saved her home from the swans, but she had forgotten to practice for the ballet performance!

She closed her eyes and made her final wish.
"I wish to be a ballerina in *Swan Lake*!"

When Leah opened her eyes, she was standing on a rock, surrounded by lily pads. Her backyard had been transformed into a giant lake!

She looked around. "This is beautiful, but I wanted to dance like the ballerina from *Swan Lake,* not have an actual lake."

Shine hung her head. "Sorry, Leah. I didn't mean to make such a big mistake."

Leah hugged Shine. "It's okay. No mistake is too big to fix. Even one as big as a lake!"

Leah started to inch off the rock. "Let's get back to dry land so we can practice spinning!" Suddenly, she slipped!

As Leah fell, she bounced off a lily pad and did a perfect ballerina spin!

"I don't know if you meant to do that, but it was amazing!" said Shine.

Leah kept bouncing and spinning from pad to pad. The swans did the same.

"If I practice more," she said, "maybe I'll finally spin like the Swan Queen!"

For the rest of the afternoon, Leah, the genies, and the swans practiced ballet on the lily pads.

Late in the day, Zac poked his head through a loose board in the fence. Shimmer and Shine quickly hid, but he didn't even notice them.

"Whoa!" he shouted to Leah. "There's a lake in your backyard!"

Zac had been practicing his leaps and was ready for the show. "You've got everything we need— the swans, the Swan Lake, and the Swan Queen!"

"I'm still missing one more piece." Leah held out her hand. "The best leaper ever! Wanna dance?" Together the two friends put on a magical performance!

After the show, Leah found Shimmer and Shine.
"We fixed our mistakes, and the day turned out great!"
She hugged the two genies. "See you tomorrow?"

"Abso-*genie*-lutely!" chimed Shimmer and Shine.

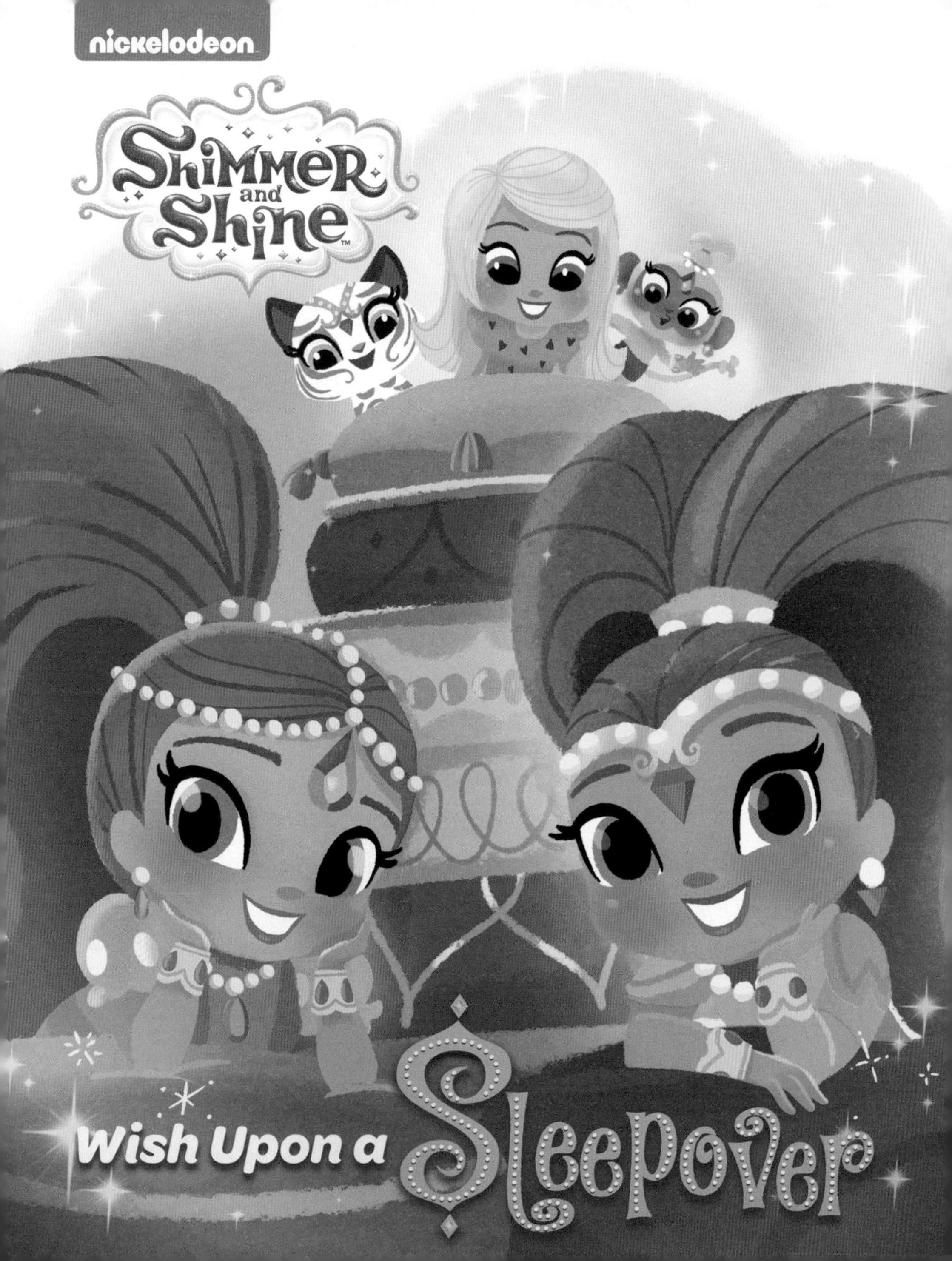
nickelodeon
Shimmer and Shine
Wish Upon a Sleepover

One evening, Shimmer and Shine were getting ready for their first sleepover party with Leah.

"Don't forget the important stuff!" Shine told her sister. "Like our miner helmet and snorkel—in case Leah wants to go deep-sea gold mining!"

Meanwhile, Leah was putting the finishing touches on her pillow fort. After placing the last pillow, it was time to call the genies!

Leah rubbed her necklace. *"Shimmer and Shine, my genies divine! Through this special chant, three wishes you'll grant!"*

Poof! The genies and their pets appeared in Leah's room—right on top of the pillow fort. "Talk about a soft landing!" laughed Shimmer.

"Welcome to the sleepover party!" said Leah.

In a burst of sparkles, Shimmer and Shine changed into their pajamas.

"Now, how does this sleepover thing work?" asked Shine. "Do we sleep *over* things, like *over* this bed?"

"Actually, a sleepover is a party where you sleep at a friend's house," explained Leah. "And there's pizza. And music and dancing!"

"And we get to sleep in a pillow fort!" Leah added. "Well . . . we were going to."

"Don't worry, Leah. We can build a new one!" Shimmer scratched her head. "Um, what *is* a pillow fort?"

Leah showed the genies how to stack pillows to make a fort. But when they were done, the fort was too small! They needed more pillows.

Shine had an idea—Leah could use her first wish!

"For my first wish," Leah said, "I wish for more pillows!"

"*Boom, Zahramay! First wish of the day!*"
chanted Shine.

Suddenly, pillows were everywhere, filling
the room from floor to ceiling!

"Is this enough?" Shimmer asked.

Leah looked at the towering piles of pillows. "When I wished for more pillows, I was thinking six or seven, not a whole roomful."

Shine smiled bashfully. "My mistake."

"It's okay, Shine. I should have told you how many I wanted." Leah handed Shine a pillow. "Now we can try building again."

Leah concentrated on making a fort. When she
turned around to show the genies, she gasped. "Whoa!"

Shimmer and Shine had used their magic
to turn the whole bedroom into a gigantic
pillow fort!

After playing in the fort, Leah and the genies were ready to dance.

Leah tried to put on some tunes, but she discovered that her music player was broken.

"I guess we can't have a dance party after all," she sighed.

"There's no such thing as *can't* when you still have wishes left!" Shine said with a twinkle in her eye.

"Okay," Leah said. "For my second wish, I wish we could play music!"

Shimmer spun her bracelets. *"Boom, Zahramay! Second wish of the day!"*

In a puff of smoke, the girls found themselves surrounded by musical instruments!

Leah plucked a guitar string. "I didn't mean to wish for instruments. I just wanted my music player to work. But maybe we can make our own music for the dance party!"

"A little magic will help us sound perfect." Shimmer sprinkled pink dust over the instruments. They began to play a rocking beat!

In a shower of blue dust, Shine turned Leah's carpet into a light-up dance floor. The dance party was on!

"This is a blast!" Leah said with a giggle. "I wish the dancing would never stop!"

Shine clapped her hands. *"Boom, Zahramay! Third wish of the day!"*

Leah laughed as she and the genies strutted around on the dance floor. "I didn't mean to make that wish, but I love this mistake!"

As the night went on, however, the girls grew tired.
"We need to stop dancing, but there are no wishes
left!" said Leah.

Shine was pooped, too. "Even my ears are tired,"
she said, picking up a pillow. "I'm going to give them
a rest." She held a pillow over each ear, and the sound
of music faded away.

"Shine, you've stopped dancing!" exclaimed Leah.

That gave Leah an idea! She reached for a pillow and threw it onto the drums. "Everybody pile the pillows on the instruments!"

The genies and their pets tossed pillows left and right. With a magical wave, Shimmer collapsed the pillow fort onto the instruments. The music stopped—and so did the dancing!

Leah hugged the two genies. "We fixed our mistakes, and the night turned out great!"

Shine yawned. "And now it's time to get some *sleep* at this sleepover!"

It was a lovely beach day! Leah was collecting pretty shells and putting them in her bucket. She was going to make jewelry. Zac was looking for a spiky pink shell so he could make a sound like a horn.

"I heard if you blow into it, you can call a pirate ship!" he said.

Zac spotted the perfect shell . . . but he'd have to wrestle it away from a crab!

While Zac chased the crab, a giant wave washed away Leah's bucket!

"My treasures!" Leah gasped. "Now what am I going to make jewelry with?"

Suddenly, she had an idea—she would use a wish to find her beach treasures! She called to her genies-in-training, **Shimmer** and **Shine**.

The genies arrived with their pets, Tala and Nahal.
"If we'd known we were going to the beach," said
Shine, "we would've worn our swimsuits, too!" But
with two claps, the genies were in their bathing suits.
"For my first wish," Leah said, "I wish I could find
more beach treasures!"

Shine clapped her hands again.
"Boom, Zahramay! First wish of
the day!"

"Is this a . . . treasure map?" asked Leah.

Shine beamed. "Yup! A map to beach treasures!"

"But I was hoping the treasures would just appear," said Leah.

Shine smiled sheepishly. "Sorry, Leah."

"It's okay," Leah said. "Sometimes mistakes happen. At least with this one, we get to go on a treasure hunt!"
Leah and the genies followed the map into a cave.

It was very dark in the cave. Shine clanged her bracelets together and the crystals on the walls twinkled with light!

Leah read the first clue. "'Watch the step down below. Through a tunnel you will go.'" She frowned. "But all I see are these giant crystals."

Just then, the floor opened,
and Leah and the genies slid

DOWNNN!

"Looks like we found the
tunnel!" laughed Shine.

The girls landed with a thump . . . across from a giant ship!

Shimmer gasped. "Oh my genie, a pirate ship!"

"The same ship as the one on the map," said Leah. "Let's swim over!"

Shimmer dipped a toe into the water and shivered. "Swimming's out, unless we want to turn into icicles."

Shine spotted Tala monkeying around on a vine. "We can swing across on these vines!"

Leah and the genies
swung from vine to vine until they reached
the pirate ship.

With a poof of magic, Shimmer and Shine
made pirate outfits appear on everyone. Now
they were ready to hunt for pirate treasure!

Leah read the next clue. "'Set your sail, point it west. Then you'll find your treasure chest.'"

"Let's get moving!" cheered Shine.

"Okay," said Leah. "For my second wish, I wish this ship would move!"

Shimmer clapped her hands. *"Boom, Zahramay! Second wish of the day!"*

A gust of wind filled the sails—and blew the treasure map into the water!

Shimmer shook her head. "Looks like I made the wind a little *too* windy."

"It's okay. You tried really hard, and you did get us moving," said Leah.

With a bit of fancy steering, the friends got the map back.

Leah tried to read the next clue, but
the water had smudged the map!
"I wish someone would just tell us
where the treasure is," sighed Leah.

"Shimmer and Shine, someone tell us divine!" chanted Shine.
A loud squawk filled the air. It was a pirate's parrot!
"He's here to tell us where the treasures are!" said Shine.
Shimmer walked toward some vines. "Maybe it's this way."
"Cold!" shouted the parrot.

Leah turned toward a large rock.
"Hot!" squawked the parrot.

Leah realized something. "He's playing the hot-and-cold game. When we're close to the treasure, he'll say 'Hot!' But when we're far away, he'll say 'Cold!'"

"Hot! Hot! Hot!"

squawked the parrot as Leah approached the rock.

The friends lifted the rock and found a chest filled with riches! "Look at all these treasures!" exclaimed Leah. "I can't believe we found them!"

Leah and the genies headed back to the beach to make jewelry with their beach treasures.

Leah gave Shimmer and Shine two sparkly necklaces. "These are for my favorite genies!"

"Thanks, Leah," said Shimmer. "We'll treasure our treasures forever!"

Just then, Zac returned. The genies and their pets quickly hid behind a sand castle so he wouldn't see them.

Leah grabbed a pink shell and handed it to him. "I don't know if it'll call a pirate ship . . . but give it a try."

Zac took a deep breath and blew. *Toot!*

The pirate ship appeared—with a little magical help from Shine.

Zac ran to check it out. "Holy horsefeathers— a pirate ship!"

Leah giggled when the two sand-covered genies popped out from behind the sand castle.

"It's a good thing we made mistakes—or we wouldn't have gone on a treasure hunt!" said Leah.

"And you wouldn't have made us these!" said Shimmer, touching her necklace.

"Exactly!" Leah said. "We fixed our mistakes, and the day turned out great!"